Snow Blind

by Ben Bo

Series Editors: Steve Barlow and Steve Skidmore

Heinemann

Published by Heinemann Educational Publishers
Halley Court, Jordan Hill, Oxford OX2 8EJ
A division of Reed Educational and Professional Publishing Ltd

OXFORD   MELBOURNE   AUCKLAND
JOHANNESBURG   BLANTYRE   GABORONE
IBADAN   PORTSMOUTH NH (USA)   CHICAGO

05   04   03   02   01
10   9   8   7   6   5   4   3   2   1
ISBN 0 435 21506 X

Illustrations by Mike Perkins
Cover design by Shireen Nathoo Design
Cover photo by Corbis/Ales Fevzer
Designed by Artistix, Thame, Oxon
Printed and bound in Great Britain by Athenaeum Press Ltd

Tel: 01865 888058   www.heinemann.co.uk

Contents

CHAPTER 1

Travis was being dead serious as usual.

'Yaaaaaaaaaaaaaaaaaaaaaaaaaaaaaa-

hoooooooooooooooooooooooooooo!'

You could hear Travis's shout echoing
all over Snowcat Mountain.

Further down the slope, Davo was ready
with the video camera.

Travis went over the edge. Full speed. No fear. The snow fizzed off his snowboard as he made the jump. He flew through the air as if he had suddenly grown wings. Twisting. Turning. Then swooping down.

'One life! No fear!' Travis was laughing now.

His board thumped on the slope. He cut a turn, spraying Davo with snow.

'Hey! Watch the camera!' Davo said.

'Did you get it, man?' Travis asked, as he slid to a stop. 'Did you get a good shot of me? I was *awesome*!'

'My Dad will go tonto if anything happens to this video,' Davo said. He wiped the snow off the camera with the sleeve of his ski jacket.

'You worry too much,' Travis said. He grabbed the camera.

Some girls were waiting by the ski lift. Travis tried to make them laugh. He held the camera at arm's length and filmed himself fooling around.

'My name is Travis Johns!' he said, 'I'm the best. I'm a legend. A snow god. And this video is going to prove it...'

'Dream on!' Davo laughed.

Travis did. Nothing was going to stop him. *Nothing.*

Same old Travis. Tall, no fear Travis. He was too busy dreaming about the Big Time to think about anything else. Too busy living to think about dying.

But all that was *before* he met Mr Glitzman.

CHAPTER 2

HARVEY J. GLITZMAN
TALENT SCOUT

That's what the sign on Mr Glitzman's door said. His office wasn't in the best part of town. It was in the worst. But Travis didn't seem to notice. He just stood outside. Smiling in his beanie hat, shades and snow jacket. Proud of his old snowboard with the skull and crossbones painted on it.

'Just keep the video rolling,' Travis told Davo. 'I want my future fans to see this.'

But Travis's break into the Big Time didn't quite go the way he planned.

CHAPTER 3

'Quit wasting my time, kid!' Mr Glitzman
said. 'I don't want to know!'

'But...' Travis started to argue.

Mr Glitzman was sitting with his feet up
on his desk. He was watching TV. And he
didn't look at all happy to see Travis, Davo
or their video camera.

'Don't mind Davo,' Travis said. 'He's with me. We're making a film.'

'I don't care if he's Stephen Spielberg,' Mr Glitzman said. '*Nobody* uses a video here!'

'But it's all about me,' Travis said. 'I'm Travis Johns – the next big American snowboard star!'

Mr Glitzman sighed. 'I wish I had a dollar for every kid who has told me that.'

'But I'll prove it if...'

'I know!' Mr Glitzman said. 'You want me to help you. You want me to be your agent. Make you a star. Make you rich.'

'Right!' said Travis.

'Wrong!' said Mr Glitzman.

Travis looked as if he had been smacked in the mouth.

'Unless...' Mr Glitzman said. A greedy look came into his eye. 'Unless you pay my fee – $500 up front – for expenses.'

'500 bucks!' Travis gasped.

'Take it or leave it, kid!' Mr Glitzman said. 'I see twenty hot-shot snowboarders like you every week.'

'But I'm better than them!' said Travis.

Mr Glitzman shook his head. 'Listen kid, if you want to make the Big Time then you'll have to pay,' he said. 'Either that or show me you're different. And that means doing something big – something *life and death*. You got that?'

Travis nodded.

'Good!' Mr Glitzman said, 'because my time costs money, kid!'

Then it was all over and Mr Glitzman was pushing them out onto the street.

'I'm not a kid!' Travis muttered as he turned away.

CHAPTER 4

That night the storm broke. The wind blew
up, suddenly, and with it came snow – lots
of snow.

Travis walked up and down his room.
Five steps one way. Turn. Five steps back.
He stopped each time he passed the window
and looked out.

The wind was whirling the snow about.
The flakes became patterns in the glow
from the street lights. These ghostly shapes
played tricks on Davo's eyes. They gave him
the creeps.

Davo had the video camera set up in

Travis's room. Travis said he wanted his future fans to see him hanging out – cool. But Travis wasn't acting so cool now. He kept walking up and down saying, 'How am I going to find that kind of money?'

'You are going to wear a hole in that rug,' said Davo.

'Shhhhhhhh!' Travis hissed. 'Can't you see I'm trying to think?'

Davo didn't like the sound of that. 'Think? Think about what?'

'About how I'm going to make Mr Glitzman change his mind,' Travis said.

'But you heard him,' said Davo.

'I heard!' Travis nodded. 'He said I was nothing special. He said he sees loads of hot-shot snowboarders just like me every week.'

'Exactly,' Davo said. 'And he wants $500 you haven't got.'

But Travis wasn't going to give up that easily. 'Then I'll just have to *show* him I'm the best!' he said. 'I'll do something big. Something *life and death*, just like Mr Glitzman said. Then he'll have to change his mind!'

As he spoke, ghostly shapes gathered at the window again. This time they were grinning at Travis, as if they knew something he didn't.

CHAPTER 5

After two days, the storm blew itself out.

By then, Travis had made up his mind.

'You're joking – right?' Davo gasped.

But Travis wasn't laughing.

'Not the Icewall!' said Davo. 'Not after heavy snow! It's *crazy*!'

'That's why I have to do it!' Travis said. 'Because it's *life and death*. Because no one else would dare. And *you* are coming with me.'

'No way!' Davo shook his head.

'How else am I going to video it so Mr Glitzman can see how good I am?' said Travis.

He had it all worked out. He was going to be famous.

'*Dead* famous, more like,' Davo said as they caught the ski lift up the mountain.

The chair creaked as it swung on its cable. Travis filmed the snow, rocks and pine trees below. The mountain was silent in the mist. Icy. Dangerous.

But Travis was blind to the danger.

They reached the end of the line. The ski lift went no higher and they got off the chair together. Their snowboards cut into snow, as they slid to a halt by a ski guide's hut.

'We'll have to walk the rest of the way,'
Travis said.

Davo looked around. A few die-hard
skiers and snowboarders were over by the
hut. They were listening to the ski guide.

'No one goes higher than this point
today,' the guide was saying. 'It's too
dangerous up there. We are going to have to
clear the snow with ice-busters. So stay
away from the Icewall. We could have an
avalanche up there at any time.'

'Ice-busters! Did you hear that?' Davo
said. 'We are talking bombs here!'

'Like I said – you worry too much!'
Travis unclipped his snowboard and picked
it up.

'I've got a bad feeling about this!' said
Davo. But he followed Travis all the same.

CHAPTER 6

It was easy to sneak past the ski guide. He was too busy to notice Travis and Davo. They ignored all the danger signs and began to climb up through the deep snow between the rocks and trees.

'Travis! Wait for me!' Davo called.

The snow crunched softly as his boots sank in. It came up over his knees with every step. Soon he passed another sign. He dug away the snow and read the warning:

DANGER! AVALANCHES.

Ahead, Travis had stopped suddenly. He was standing by a pine tree, near some big rocks. Something was wrong.

'What is it?' Davo asked, catching up.

'The Icewall!' The words were just breath on Travis's lips.

Davo looked down. He was standing right on the edge. In front of him the ground just fell away to nothing. The drop dragged his gaze down so fast, it made his head spin. Dizzy, he stepped back quickly.

It was awesome. From where they stood, they could see it all. The Icewall was 100 metres wide, maybe more. Almost a sheer drop. A white wall of ice and snow.

'You can video it all from here,' Travis said. He tossed the camera to Davo and laughed. 'One life! No fear – right!'

'Right,' said Davo, feeling sick.

CHAPTER 7

Davo watched as Travis climbed right up to the top of the Icewall. He saw Travis wave and then move on out of sight.

Davo felt alone. He stood by the pine tree and waited, hoping that Travis might change his mind and come back down.

But Travis didn't.

Davo noticed some people on the mountain above the Icewall. They were high up and far away, so he couldn't see what they were doing. Soon after that, a helicopter swooped low over the mountain and he watched it turn and fly on.

He was alone again. Watching. Waiting. Tied to that tree by his promise to Travis. And all the while Davo wondered what he was doing up there. Why had he come?

'It's all *Mr Glitzman's* fault!' he spat.

'*Glitzman-Glitzman-Glitzman.*' His own voice echoed back at him.

The sound made Davo jump. He looked around. And suddenly he could see faces all around him. Ghostly faces in the rocks and in the trees. Faces frozen in the ice and snow. They were just like the ones he had seen at Travis's window, only now they were all the same. They all looked just like Mr Glitzman.

It was as if a hundred Mr Glitzmans had followed them to see what would happen.

'They aren't real!' Davo told himself. But he could have sworn he heard an echo of Mr Glitzman's voice on the wind.

'*Life and death!*' that voice whispered.

And suddenly, Davo was scared. Dead scared.

CHAPTER 8

'Travis! No!' Davo's shout came too late.

'Yaaaaaaaaaaaaaaaaaaaaaaaaaaaaaaa-hoooooooooooooooooooooooooooooo!'

Travis's voice echoed all around.

'He's going to do it!' Davo said. He struggled to get the video camera to his eye. He zoomed in on the slope above, just as Travis made the jump.

Travis hit the edge and burst into the air in a blur of snow. He flew high over the Icewall, surfing on thin air. And, in that moment, it seemed there was nothing he could not do.

As Travis rocketed into the air, he was already spinning. He bent his knees and grabbed the edge of his board. He tucked his head down and began to roll. Head over heels. For a slow-motion moment, he was upside down over the Icewall.

It was awesome. Full-on. A no-prisoners kind of jump and Davo filmed it all.

Travis eased himself upright again. He let his own weight pull him out of the turn. A moment later, he was coming in to land. Then suddenly, Travis was flashing down the Icewall. It was a breathless slide. It was an icy glide. It was a deadly snow ride. Down, down, down. Faster and faster.

'He isn't going to make it!' Davo gasped.

Travis cut across the Icewall towards him. He slashed a turn, and timed it just right as he came off the Icewall. He dug in the edge of his board, sending a great wave of snow flying, as he came to a stop.

Travis threw back his head and whooped at the sky. 'I did it! I beat the Icewall!'

Suddenly, they were both laughing. Shouting. Yelling with relief. And, just for a second, it seemed as if it was all over. Just for a second, it seemed Travis had taken on the Icewall and won.

Then they heard the warning.

CHAPTER 9

It sounded like a blast on a truck's horn. One long warning note. It was a spooky sound, as if somewhere a wolf was howling.

Travis looked up. 'Ice-busters!' he said.

Then Davo remembered the ski guide's warning and suddenly he understood. The people he had seen on the mountain above had been putting down ice-busters. The helicopter had been checking the slopes were clear. And now they were about to set off an avalanche to clear the snow.

'They don't know we're here!' Davo said. He grabbed his snowboard and pushed his feet into the bindings.

But it was already too late.

On the slope high above, there was a sudden puff of snow. It looked like a mini fountain, a burst of white. Then there was another. And another. The ice-busters went off one by one.

As the echoes died, the snow on the slopes above began to crumble. It just started falling away. Small pieces at first, then larger chunks. Then the white mass broke up. And suddenly, it seemed as if the whole side of the mountain was on the move.

'Awesome, man!' yelled Travis. He grabbed the video camera and filmed it all. 'Mr Glitzman is going to love this!'

What had once been smooth and white was now changing fast. The snow began to slip down the mountain side. Within a few metres the avalanche was moving very fast. Soon it would be going at over 100 kilometres an hour. It burst over the top of the Icewall and rushed down the slope towards them.

For the first time, Davo saw fear in Travis's eyes.

'We have to get to the rocks!' Travis had to shout above the roar of the avalanche.

The rocks were their only hope of shelter. Travis was closer.

'You can make it!' Davo shouted.

Travis shook his head. 'Not without you!'

The avalanche was almost on them now. It ate up everything in its path – the rocks and trees and sky. And it shook the mountain with its terrible noise.

Travis looked at Davo. 'No fear, right?'

Davo knew what Travis meant. He nodded, 'Right!'

Together they turned their snowboards down the mountain. Side by side, the two friends shot down the slope. But they could not escape that deadly wave of snow.

Davo was the first to fall. The snow just closed in around him. It knocked him down. But even as he fell, he saw Travis riding on. Travis seemed to be flying, like a snow god surfing on a storm of snow.

Then Davo hit the ground. He hit hard and went sliding on down the slope. The avalanche swept him on until he thought he would never stop.

And it all might have ended there for Davo. He might have stayed high up on Snowcat Mountain forever, had the avalanche not thrown him aside.

It all happened so fast. One moment he was falling, the next he was being pushed clear. The main force of the snow roared past. He slid to a stop and gulped for breath. Then he got to his knees and looked around.

'Traaaaaaaaaaviiiiiiiiiiiiiiiiiiiiiiiis!'

Davo's shout echoed all around Snowcat Mountain.

CHAPTER 10

That's how it ended – the video Travis and Davo made. The one Davo brought down from Snowcat Mountain. The one Travis always said would prove he was *the best*.

And the next day Davo made Mr Glitzman watch it all. He stood in that office until the TV screen went blank.

'That's it. There isn't any more,' Davo said. 'You've seen it all now.'

Mr Glitzman was sitting behind his desk, staring at the screen.

Davo took the tape out of the video machine. His hands were shaking. He stood staring at that small black box. Inside, were all Travis's hopes, all Travis's dreams.

'Yeah! I remember him now!' Mr Glitzman said. 'Tall kid. Thought he was a hot-shot. He came to see me a couple of days ago. And I told him to...'

Davo nodded. 'Yes. He did everything you told him to,' he said. 'Here's the proof.'

Davo put the video down on Mr Glitzman's desk.

'Stop messing with me, kid! There has to be more,' Mr Glitzman said. 'Tell me what happened! Tell me where I can find Travis Johns!'

Mr Glitzman was sweating now.

Davo just turned away.

'Please! This is important, kid!' Mr Glitzman begged. 'This Travis could go far, if he had an agent like *me*. We're talking the Big Time. Mega-deals. Mega-bucks.'

Davo reached the door and stopped. Just for a moment, he pictured Travis on his snowboard – laughing, free.

'Tell that to Travis!' Davo said. 'You'll find him up on Snowcat Mountain. Right up near the top. Where he always wanted to be.'